The Ghost Writer

A Play in Two Acts

by

Stephen Evans

"Yet but three? Come one more."

William Shakespeare

A Midsummer Night's Dream

For production permissions and rights, contact the playwright.

The Ghost Writer: Stephen Evans 2nd Edition

ISBN: 978-1-953725-23-3

Cast of Characters

KATE: A successful agent and attorney. She's fortyish, very bright, and passionate beneath hard-won knowledge.

MICHAEL: A gifted playwright who has never reached his artistic potential. 35 years old, he is Kate's current lover.

HARRY: A legendary New York producer struggling to regain his magic touch. Harry is a cross between Harold Hill and Harry Houdini. He is a survivor with a golden glint in his eye. At 60 years old, he is energetic, unprincipled, sexy, and Kate's ex.

WILL: The Ghost Writer.

Scene

A theater.

Time

The present.

ACT I Scene 1

Setting: A Broadway theater. Upstage
center a door is built into the
set.

At Rise: The set is decorated with
decorated with banners,
streamers, and balloons for an
opening night party. But the
stage is empty of people. Set
pieces are scattered and
overturned. Something bad has
happened here.

*Kate enters through the door, closing it
tightly. She takes off her coat, revealing a
glamorous evening gown. She throws her
coat over an upside-down chair, then
turns a table upright and sets out a bottle
of champagne and three glasses. She pops
open the champagne and pours all three.*

*Kate re-enters and begins, with obvious
joy, to take down the decorations,
stopping to pop a couple of balloons.*

The door swings slowly open. She looks offstage.

KATE

Michael?

Hearing no answer, she goes to the door, looks out and sees no one. She closes it firmly, then returns to the decorations, popping the last balloon.

The door slowly swings open again. More nervous, she goes to the door and looks out again.

KATE

Harry?

Again there's no answer. She again closes the door firmly, checks to make sure.

KATE

So may these outward shows be least themselves,
the world is still deceived by ornaments.

Puzzled, and unable to understand why she has said these words, Kate leans with her back against the door. She hears turns her head to watch the knob on the door turn slowly, and the door inch open- creaking, naturally. She forces herself to look.

Michael's head appears in the doorway.
They see each other and scream.)

KATE

Michael!

Michael looks around the set nervously.

MICHAEL

Is it safe?

KATE

It's 1:00 A.M. in New York City. You want safe, move to Connecticut.

Michael removes his coat, stands up an overturned coat rack, and hangs his coat up. He stares out into the audience.

MICHAEL

They'll hunt us down eventually.

KATE

Who?

MICHAEL

The audience.

KATE

There is that possibility. But you know what Harry says.

Imitating Harry's voice.

Never blame the audience, kid. All they do is sit there.

MICHAEL

That's true. That's all they did. Sit there. And sit there. And sit there. I think they may have stopped breathing. How much could you sit through?

KATE

About the first three hours.

MICHAEL

That was decent of you.

KATE

Well, I wanted to see how the first act ended.

MICHAEL

As I recall, in flames.

KATE

I would have stayed until the final curtain, but I forgot to pack a suitcase.

MICHAEL

Some agent. Opening night of my show and you won't even lie about how bad it is.

KATE

Can you call it an opening when it closes the same night?

MICHAEL

You're not helping.

She brings him a drink.

KATE

Anyway, I prefer the term personal representative. And be nice to me. I may have to support you.

MICHAEL

A few more of these and you'll definitely have to support me.

KATE

So. How do you feel?

MICHAEL

The same way I felt the last two times. Except I'm better at it with practice.

KATE

Makes sense.

MICHAEL

You know, at first, it was fine. People were enjoying themselves, smiling and laughing. I thought, this isn't so bad. And then it happened. Something that made my blood run cold.

KATE

What?

MICHAEL

The curtain went up.

KATE

Is there anything I can do?

MICHAEL
Could you shoot Harry?

KATE
I'm all out of silver bullets.

MICHAEL
Never mind.

KATE
*Not listening, caught up in
the idea*
We could try a stake through his heart.

MICHAEL
Forget it.

KATE
But I doubt we could find it.

MICHAEL
I'm sorry I brought it up.

KATE
What?

MICHAEL
Just, thanks for listening.

KATE
That's what I'm here for.

MICHAEL
And thanks for not saying I told you so.

KATE
It never entered my mind.

*She unveils a banner saying: I Told You
So!*

MICHAEL

Nice.

KATE

I saved it from the last time.

MICHAEL

I thought it looked familiar.

KATE

As far as I'm concerned, this is the best thing
that could have happened, to both of us. You
promised that if this show wasn't successful,
you and I would go away together. Somewhere
far away where you can get back to doing your
kind of writing.

MICHAEL

Great. We're moving to Disneyland.

KATE

Almost. I was thinking maybe L.A. You could
try screenwriting.

MICHAEL

Hollywood. What a concept! There would be
no limit to the amount of money I could
squander.

KATE

I'm serious. You should think about it.
Actually, I've been thinking about it for a
while now. I've been offered an executive
position with a studio—top budgets, choice of
projects, everything I could want. And they
said I could bring you in with me.

MICHAEL

I see.

KATE

So, what do you think?

MICHAEL

Are you going?

KATE

I asked what you think?

MICHAEL

I think you should go.

KATE

I see. What about you?

MICHAEL

I'm a playwright.

KATE

Look, I know lately things haven't been right
between us.

MICHAEL

That has nothing to do with it.

KATE

Maybe, with a fresh start somewhere...

MICHAEL

Kate, I wish I could tell you what you want to hear. You deserve it. But I can't.

KATE

Okay, maybe you could teach, I don't know. The important thing is that we'll be there, and Harry won't.

MICHAEL

You can't blame this all on Harry.

KATE

Why not? Everyone else does. Admit it: If it wasn't for Harry, you never would have touched the kind of material I saw tonight. I don't understand how he talks people into these things. Not just you- everybody, including me. I've been with him since I got out of law school, and I can't tell you why I put up with it.

MICHAEL

I can. There are two reasons.

KATE

Enlighten me.

MICHAEL

First, he used to be one of the most successful producers on Broadway.

KATE
Ancient history. What's the second reason?

MICHAEL
The second reason you know as well as I do.
He can make anything sound reasonable. He
could sell weight loss centers in Third World
countries. In fact, I think he tried it.

KATE
That is exactly why you have to get away from
him. He is manipulative, insensitive, and
totally without any sense of decency.

MICHAEL
I like him too.

KATE
Michael, I know he's your oldest friend. He's
mine, too. But you've outgrown him. It's time
to move on.

MICHAEL
I know. I know.
                She looks at him skeptically.
I know!

KATE
Promise me you'll tell him tonight?

MICHAEL
I promise.

KATE

Then let's break out the champagne. We have
something to celebrate after all.

At this point, Harry bursts in. He too is in
formal attire, though his is rumpled.

HARRY

Break out the champagne! We have something
to celebrate after all.

MICHAEL

What are you talking about?

HARRY

The show, of course. A triumph of the first
magnitude.

They stare at him.

HARRY

Okay, maybe not the first magnitude. But a
triumph, nonetheless.

MICHAEL

You really have lost it this time, Harry. The
show was a disaster. It sank with all hands.
There were no survivors.

HARRY

You're over-reacting.

MICHAEL

Were you at the same opening night I was?

KATE

Can you call it an opening when it closes the same night?

MICHAEL

You're not helping!

KATE

Sorry.
Bringing them each a glass of champagne

KATE

Here. This is the extent of my commiseration for tonight.

KATE
To Harry
If you need me, I'll be in the office working on your bankruptcy. Take your time. By the way, watch out for that curtain.

She exits.

MICHAEL

Now you tell me.

HARRY

I still don't think it was that bad. During the first act, people were smiling and laughing.

MICHAEL

They were throwing paper airplanes at the actors.

HARRY

Then at intermission, half the audience left.

MICHAEL
The lucky half.

HARRY
Maybe their babysitters had to be home early.

MICHAEL
I've heard babysitters have a very strong
union.

HARRY
I'm just trying to cheer you up.

He makes another drink, very strong, and
gives it to Michael

HARRY
Actually, Mike, I wasn't going to tell you this
until tomorrow. But, in my professional
judgment based on my 33 years on Broadway...

MICHAEL
Yes?

HARRY
The show was a disaster. It sank with all hands.
There were no survivors.

MICHAEL
An eloquent eulogy to an excruciating
evening.

HARRY
Now we can't take this too hard.

MICHAEL

You know, that's true. No matter how hard we take this, it's not too hard.

HARRY

That's not what I mean. Theater is a risky business.

MICHAEL

What business? All we do is lose money. It's more like a charity program for lawyers.

HARRY

With a lawyer like Kate, is that so bad?
Puzzled
She seems to be taking this rather well.

MICHAEL

She's imagining how many people are going to sue us in the morning. And she's also thinking that I'll be able to stay home now and clean the apartment. This is the most depressing night of my life since our last opening night. I hate feeling like this. Why do we do it, anyway? Why do we put ourselves through this?

HARRY

Maybe we could write a book about it.

MICHAEL

There's something very wrong with the whole process.

HARRY
We could write a book about the whole
process.

MICHAEL
Maybe we're fooling ourselves.

HARRY
We could write a book about fools.

MICHAEL
Maybe the magic is gone.

HARRY
We could call it Magic Fools.

MICHAEL
All the pain and the suffering and the lost
time. That's the worst. The time.

HARRY
*Harry looks at Michael's
watch*
2:15. Or maybe we could open a clinic for
failures.

MICHAEL
Time and failure.

HARRY
Our motto could be: Nobody knows failure
like we do.

MICHAEL
Nobody knows the trouble I've seen. Nothing
ever seems to work out right anymore. We
should have known. We did know. But still we
wasted all that money, all that- time.

HARRY
*Again Harry looks at
Michael's watch*
2:16. We could have counseling centers across
the country. Failures Anonymous. Or, Failure
Associates. How do you do, I'm Harry
Skidmore, senior failure consultant.

MICHAEL
The question is: Why?

HARRY
What?

MICHAEL
What?

HARRY
What did you say?

MICHAEL
I said why?

HARRY
Oh.
Pause
Why what?

MICHAEL

Let's work backwards on this one. You said
why what to my what asking what you said
which means that you said why what to my
original why meaning that you want to know
why I said why?

Pause

HARRY

What?

MICHAEL

I thought it was perfectly clear.

Pause

HARRY

What?

MICHAEL

What I said.

HARRY

Which what?

MICHAEL

No, we're entering a whole new dimension
here. We'd better quit while we're ahead.

Pause

HARRY

Ahead of what?

MICHAEL
Let me put it this way: Why do...we do...what we do? I sound like Frank Sinatra.

HARRY
We do it because we have to.

MICHAEL
Why?

HARRY
Why what?

MICHAEL
Don't start that again. Why do we have to do it?

HARRY
We need to.

MICHAEL
But why?

HARRY
*Slightly annoyed by the
obviousness of it all*
To live out the fullest expression of our lives, making each act a tiny catalyst in the combustion of infinite beauty.

MICHAEL
Oh. Did you make that up?

HARRY
I think it was in a Lite Beer commercial.

MICHAEL

Why did I ask?

HARRY

Ask what? Just kidding! Anyway it's a stupid question. There is no "why". We do it because it's what we do. I am a producer. You are a writer. So, we produce and write.

MICHAEL

How simple life is for the tautologically challenged. In that case, I have another question: what do we do now?

HARRY

We move on.

MICHAEL

No.

HARRY

Continue.

MICHAEL

Sorry.

HARRY

Try, try again?

MICHAEL

Wrong. Harry, sit down.

HARRY
He is sitting

Okay.

MICHAEL

I've been meaning to talk to you about this for a long time, but I could never figure out how to say it.

HARRY

You can say anything to me.

MICHAEL

Okay. Harry, this is the third time in a row that we have failed to keep a show open past opening night. I think that's a clue. Someone is telling us to stop.

HARRY

Yeah, the New York Times.

Michael reacts.

HARRY

Sorry. So we've hit a few rough spots. It happens to everyone. You can't forget everything we've been through just because we're having an off period.

MICHAEL

We're not having an off period. We're off. Period. And I haven't forgotten what you and I been through together. It was a miracle. But one miracle is all you get in life, Harry. We've had ours. We shouldn't be greedy. I mean it's not like we need the money anymore.

HARRY

Bite your tongue.

MICHAEL

But we have to face the fact that we can't
produce anything decent. We never were
artistic, but at least we were clever. Now
we're—what did they say—obvious. Mindless.
Trite. Garbage. Tell me when to stop. Let's
face it! You and I are through. I can't write
what you want anymore. I'm empty. Drained.
It's time to pack up, go home, teach freshman
English at some small Midwestern college that
does "Our Town" every spring. Don't you see?

**The weight of this sad time we must obey,
speak what we feel, not what we ought to
say.**

HARRY

There's no need to get literary. I feel bad
enough as it is.

MICHAEL

I don't know why I said that.

HARRY

You need sleep.

MICHAEL

I need time. To myself.

HARRY

We'll talk about it tomorrow. I'll fix you my
special tonic, and then you'll sleep the sleep of
the damned.

MICHAEL
It wouldn't surprise me.

HARRY
What time did I say it was?

MICHAEL
**Thou art so fat-witted with drinking of old
sack, and unbuttoning thee after supper, and
sleeping upon benches after noon, that thou
hast forgotten that which thou wouldst truly
know. What a devil hast thou to do with the
time of day? Unless hours were cups of sack
and minutes capons, and clocks the tongues
of bawds, and dials the signs of sleeping
houses, and the blessed sun himself a fair hot
wench in flame coloured taffeta, I see no
reason why thou shouldst be so superfluous
as to demand the time of day.**

HARRY
If you don't want to tell me, just say so.

MICHAEL
Henry IV, Part 1.

HARRY
What?

MICHAEL
That was Hal's speech to Falstaff in Act 1,
scene 2 of Henry IV, Part 1. Or was it Act 1,
scene 1 of Henry the IV, Part 2?

HARRY
It could be Rocky 5 for all I know.

MICHAEL
I love that speech. That's one of my favorite speeches.

HARRY
Shakespeare. Now there was a great operator.

MICHAEL
But it's not what I was going to say.

HARRY
He knew just what his audiences wanted.

MICHAEL
I once thought I was going to be the next Shakespeare.

HARRY
A little blood, a little sex, a little more blood, and he had a hit. Today he'd be the president of a network.

MICHAEL
The next Shakespeare. What a laugh.

HARRY
Too bad Old Will isn't here now. We could use a little influence. Influence...

Harry gets THE IDEA, and begins working it out, following Michael around the room as if measuring him.

MICHAEL

Lately, when I'm working, I feel like Dr. Frankenstein. Whatever I write comes sneaking up behind me with murder in its eyes.

> *Michael looks behind himself,*
> *sees Harry, and starts.*

It isn't worth it anymore, Harry. I'm going home.

HARRY

I know.

MICHAEL

I mean it. I'm heading west into the sunset.

HARRY

I think that's best. You've been through enough. Seeing your work torn apart by unfeeling audiences, insensitive critics, and, I admit it, greedy producers.

MICHAEL

You're obviously plotting something, and I don't want to know what it is. What is it?

HARRY

I'm just agreeing with you. It's time to go home.

MICHAEL

It is?

HARRY

It is. It's time to return to the source.

MICHAEL

The source?

HARRY

Yes, the source. As in:

Harry makes a big gesture

The SOURCE. We need a return to that which
made the theater great in days of yore.

MICHAEL

You mean tap-dancing?

HARRY

No. Farther yore than that.

MICHAEL

I know this is a mistake, but–what are you
talking about?

HARRY

Releasing his excitement

Mike, in a little while, people are going to be
throwing money at us. We'll have to hire
people to count the people counting it.

MICHAEL

Harry, calm down.

HARRY

Our next show will be the show of the
century!

MICHAEL

Harry, there isn't going to be a next show.
After tonight's show, they won't even let us
drive down Broadway. Besides, why would
anyone want to see a new show from us?

HARRY

Because we're not going to write it.

MICHAEL

That's a good start. Who is?

HARRY

William Shakespeare.

MICHAEL

Harry, William Shakespeare is dead.

HARRY

That's what makes it so spectacular.

MICHAEL

I can't argue with that. Well, if it's okay with
him, it's okay with me. Just remember that I'm
leaving.

HARRY

You can't leave.

MICHAEL

Why not?

HARRY

He only talks to you.

MICHAEL

Death is no excuse for being anti-social.

HARRY
Can you roll your eyes?

MICHAEL
No, but I can roll my 'R's.

HARRY
Work on it. Can you moan?

MICHAEL
This is getting personal.

HARRY
Never mind, we'll get a sound man.

MICHAEL
Neither of us will qualify.

HARRY
Now, when the reporters come–

MICHAEL
Reporters?

HARRY
The public has a right to know about
something as momentous as this. When the
reporters come, you may have to moan and
roll yours eyes at the same time. So start
practicing.
   *Michael moans and rolls his eyes in
   disbelief*

HARRY
That was good. Keep practicing.

MICHAEL

Stop. Don't say any more. I want to go back to the beginning so that I can prepare my insanity defense.

HARRY

Fair enough.

MICHAEL

Okay. Now. You and I are going to do a play, a play written by William Shakespeare.

HARRY

Not just a play. A <u>new</u> play.

MICHAEL

A new play, that no one has ever seen before, written by Shakespeare.

HARRY

Right.

MICHAEL

Only, now this is just a guess on my part, Shakespeare isn't really going to write this play.

HARRY

Right.

MICHAEL

And if Shakespeare isn't going to write this play written by Shakespeare, who is?

BOTH

You are.

MICHAEL
Right.

HARRY
I'll make it simple.

MICHAEL
I can't wait to hear this.

HARRY
You are going to write a play. A very, very
good play. The best play that anyone has
written for years and years. Real Art stuff. We
are going to tell the world that Shakespeare is
writing this play through you. A spiritual
connection. A voice from the other world. It
happens all the time. There's a woman in
England who writes music by Mozart and
Beethoven. Only she can't read a note. She just
hears it in her head.

MICHAEL
You should call her. We could do a musical.

HARRY
You know... no, next time maybe. Anyway,
this is big time stuff now. What's it called?
Tunneling.

MICHAEL
I think that's Channeling.

HARRY
Whatever. Besides, Shakespeare was always
writing about ghosts.

MICHAEL
How would you know?

HARRY
I am not totally alliterative. I'm telling you this is genius. This may be the greatest idea I have ever had.

MICHAEL
Now there's an intense competition. Harry, even you can't be serious about this.

HARRY
I know we can pull it off. You said yourself that no one would touch one of our shows. But how can they turn down Shakespeare?

MICHAEL
How are you going to get the money? Who in his or her right mind would even listen to you long enough to let you explain it?

HARRY
You.

MICHAEL
Harry, be sensible. Suppose I could write something good enough to have been written by Shakespeare. Who would believe it was his and not mine?

HARRY
Look at it this way. If you did write something that good, who would believe it was yours and not his?

MICHAEL

You've never stooped to telling the truth
before.

HARRY

I lost my head. Look at it another way.
Suppose what you write isn't so terrific. He's
been dead 500 years; he's bound to be a little
rusty.

Serious

I know we haven't done too well together
recently...

MICHAEL

Shall I count the slashes on my wrist?

HARRY

And I know it's my fault. My style just doesn't
work anymore. The audiences are different
now. They don't want what I have to give.
They see it on TV, in reruns, and they fall all
over it. But put it on Broadway... I don't know.
But I'm thinking, maybe they'll want you, if I
let you do what you do best. You deserve that
opportunity. And I need to be the one to give
it to you. Does that make sense?

MICHAEL

Yeah. I think so.

HARRY

You know, tonight I was sitting in the house
watching the show. But I couldn't keep my
mind on it.

MICHAEL
You and the first thirty rows.

HARRY
Something happened, something very small,
and now nothing's the same for me.

MICHAEL
What?

HARRY
It's silly. But I keep thinking about it. It was
during the show. I saw you.

MICHAEL
That must have been a shock.

HARRY
Demonstrating
And you took your program and folded it
down the center.

MICHAEL
Paper airplanes, I told you.

HARRY
And then you very carefully, very neatly, tore
it in half. And I knew it was the end.

MICHAEL
Harry?

HARRY

And I won't fight it, if you'll do one thing for me—let me give you this last show. Let me give you this chance. Look, we don't have to be out of here until tomorrow. What better place to write about Shakespeare than in a theater? Just try. One night.

MICHAEL

Harry?

HARRY

I'll make a deal with you. One night, and if you don't think it will work. Then I'll go. I'll... retire. You'll be free. Don't decide now. Just think about it. Okay?

MICHAEL

I'll think about it.

HARRY

Thanks. Well. I guess I better go.

MICHAEL
Meaningfully

Where will you go?

HARRY
Misunderstanding

To the library. It's time that Shakespeare and I met quill to quill.

He leaves

MICHAEL
This thought is as a death which cannot choose
But weep to have that which it fears to lose.

I think I'm having a midsummer day's nightmare.

Kate enters.

KATE
He's gone?

MICHAEL
Yes.

KATE
Was he angry?

MICHAEL
No, I wouldn't say he was angry.

KATE
Did you break it to him gently?

MICHAEL
Gently. Yeah. I'd say gently.

KATE
I'm glad you were gentle. How gentle were you?

MICHAEL
Gentle. Very gentle. Extremely gentle. So gentle that he may not even realize that I told him.

KATE

You didn't tell him.

MICHAEL

I tried. I just couldn't. You know, it took him all of three minutes to recover. He's already working on our next play. I tried to tell him. He wouldn't listen. Oh, the good part is that I'm not writing it.

KATE

Who is?

MICHAEL

Let's just say he's bringing in a ghost writer.

KATE

A ghost writer? For whom?

MICHAEL

A ghost. Harry's got this idea that I am going to collaborate with the spirit of William Shakespeare.

KATE

Michael, do you ever just stop and think?

MICHAEL

I don't think so.

KATE

I don't mean think, I mean... just let your mind go blank.

MICHAEL

Oh. Frequently.

KATE
Somebody once told me that, when you let
your mind go blank, the first thing you think
about is the thing you want most. After you let
your mind drift, what's your first thought?

MICHAEL
You.

KATE
That's a good answer. Now tell the truth.

MICHAEL
Well, if you're going to be picky... food.

KATE
Why food?

MICHAEL
My mind only goes blank when I'm hungry.

KATE
You're always hungry.

MICHAEL
My mind goes blank a lot.

KATE
Try to be serious.

MICHAEL
I'm trying.

KATE
You certainly are. Don't you ever think about
what's important to you?

MICHAEL
I did when I was young.

KATE
You're still young.

MICHAEL
I didn't say it was a long time ago.

KATE
Fine. So tell me what's important to you.
A long pause
Did you think about food again?

MICHAEL
Not until you brought it up.

KATE
I'm sorry. Don't think about food.

MICHAEL
You can't not think about something unless
you think about not thinking about it. So if I
don't think about it I'm thinking about it.

KATE
Okay, go ahead and think about it.

MICHAEL
Thanks, I'm not hungry.

KATE
You're being purposely evasive.

MICHAEL
I just can't talk about these things with you.

KATE

I see. Can you tell me why?

MICHAEL

It's like the candles on your birthday cake. You blow them out and make a wish. But if you tell anyone, it won't come true.

KATE

That's not it. I know why you won't talk to me. I know why Harry can talk you into anything. You can afford to fail by other people's standards. But you're afraid to let anyone judge you by your own. Do you know why I got into this business? Because my talent is seeing talent, and finding a way to make it grow. You have as much talent as anyone I've ever worked with, and it's all going to waste. Whose fault is that?

MICHAEL

Not yours.

KATE

Damn right it's not mine. So why is it that I can't help but blame myself? I should have kept things strictly business. Then I was just losing money.

MICHAEL

You're just soft-hearted, that's all.

KATE

About you, maybe. About nothing else in this world.

MICHAEL

How about Harry?

KATE

I said this world, not the underworld.

MICHAEL

I wish you could explain to me why you feel the way you do about him. Nobody can get to you like he can.

KATE

You do all right.

MICHAEL

No. I make you angry. Harry makes you desperate. Why?

KATE

What has he told you?

MICHAEL

Not much. He told me that one night at a party you both got drunk and you ended up sleeping together, and that you've never been the same since.

KATE

It's not true.

MICHAEL

What's not true? That you slept together or
that it was only one night? It's obvious you've
never been the same.

KATE

Stop it.

MICHAEL

Why? Feeling desperate?

KATE

If I am, it's for you.

MICHAEL

Tell me what he meant to you.

KATE

I can't.

MICHAEL

Well. I guess that makes us even. Harry will be
back here any minute now. I don't think he
realized that there are very few libraries open
at two o'clock in the morning. So, what should
I tell him? Or is there something you'd like to
tell him?

Pause

He says if I do this, he'll leave.

KATE

Maybe, in some way I don't understand, I'm
holding you back as much as he is.

MICHAEL

No. You don't know...

KATE

Just do me a favor. Don't follow him all your life. You want to know who the real ghost writer around here is? It's the one who died the day you met him.

MICHAEL

Kate, I...

There's a noise offstage, someone tripping over something.

KATE

Go to your room.

MICHAEL

Yes, Mother.

KATE

I'll handle this. I just want a little privacy.

MICHAEL
A la Groucho
Why didn't you say so?

Kate glares

MICHAEL

I'm going, I'm going.

KATE

Good idea.

He leaves. Harry enters

KATE

How was the library?

> HARRY

Closed.

> KATE

They don't keep the same hours as adult bookstores.

> HARRY

Did Mike tell you why I went to the library?

> KATE

He did.

> HARRY

What did you do with the body?

> KATE

The same thing I'm going to do with yours. Harry—

> HARRY

I know what you're going to say. You're going to say I'm a rotten devious scheming meddler who doesn't deserve to be associated with a real talent like Mike.

> KATE

Right.

> HARRY

And then you're going to say that I'm ruining his career, like I almost ruined yours.

> KATE

Exactly.

HARRY
I didn't mean to.

KATE
What am I going to do with you? You're like
the Pied Piper, Harry. These kids come to you,
fresh and eager and naive like I was, and they
follow you until they drown. I was lucky. I
learned to swim. But he won't. He'll drown
unless you help.

HARRY
Did I ever tell you how we met?

KATE
I know how we met. I was there.

HARRY
How Mike and I met.

KATE
You must have. There is very little that goes
on in your brain that doesn't eventually come
out of your mouth—

HARRY
He was still in college–

KATE
At least twice.

HARRY
It was right after you left me.

KATE
Which time?

                    HARRY
The last, I think.

                    KATE
That was my best.

                    HARRY
There was a professor who was a friend of
mine.

                    KATE
Past tense I note.

                    HARRY
Every year he'd drag me down to this little
hole in the wall theater across from the
campus to see his latest prodigy. I don't know
why I went, except you never know, right?

                    KATE
Right. You never know when you're going to
find a coed who'd just love to meet a
Broadway producer.

                    HARRY
Well, that too. It was an evening of one act
plays. I fell asleep mid-way through act one.
All of them. And then these words started
drifting in and out of my dream.

   *He pulls a crumpled piece of paper out of
   his wallet.*

HARRY

It's a little hard to read now. Where are my glasses?

He puts them on.

He said, this guy in the play said:

Reading a little but knowing a lot.

We were never happy together. Not once. At least, she was never happy with me. But I always thought that we were really happy being unhappy together. I mean, we were probably going to be unhappy anyway. So why not be unhappy with someone you love? That's what love is all about-sharing your unhappiness together.

KATE

That sounds like us.

HARRY

That's what I thought.

Pause

HARRY

Anyway, I thought, how does this kid who's never been anywhere know how I feel this exact moment? I had to meet the playwright. Anyway, what I'm really trying to say is, it's all your fault.

KATE

My fault?

HARRY

Yes. If you hadn't left me, I wouldn't have been feeling that way and I wouldn't have asked to meet him.

KATE

I see.

HARRY

I wonder what would have happened to him. You know? If I had shown up one week earlier or one week later...

KATE

We'll never know.

HARRY

I guess. I need your help, Kate. I want your help.

KATE

Is that all you want?

HARRY

It's against the rules to know what you want until it's too late to get it.

KATE

Break the rules. You're good at it.

HARRY

I used to think so. Kate, I'm trying to learn to be one of the good guys. I don't know if I can. I'm not sure why I want to. But I need help.

He takes her hand

HARRY

I need to make it up to him. I need to make it
up to me. And to you.

KATE
Calling

Michael!

He enters.

MICHAEL

No sign of a struggle.

KATE

Do you know you talk in your sleep? You do.
You talk a lot. But I can never understand the
words. And I wonder. I wonder if you're
writing in your sleep the words you should be
writing when you're awake. I know it sounds
ridiculous. But you know what's even more
ridiculous? I sit there listening, sometimes all
night, with a pencil and a notebook, trying to
catch the words. I never can. But I try. Because
I think someday I'm going to understand those
words. I'm going to write them down. And
when I do I'm going to wake you up and show
them to you, and you're going to see what you
can really do. I'd give everything for that.

MICHAEL

I don't understand...

KATE

You're doing the play.

MICHAEL
What? But you said...

KATE
I know what I said, but I've thought it over and I think you should do one more. Only this time you are going to write the right words, your words.

She turns to Harry.

KATE
From now on, I'm going to see that no one, not Harry, not me, not the Ghost of Shakespeare himself, comes between you and your work.

She turns back to Michael

KATE
I'm going to live, eat, sleep, breathe, laugh, cry, and everything else I can think of with you, until you are through with this play, and anything else that holds you to the life you're living now.
She turns back to Harry

KATE
Okay, this is the way it's going to be...

She moves away to talk to Harry. Michael looks at her

MICHAEL

Perhaps he loves you now,
and now no soil or cautel doth besmirch
the virtue of his will; but you must fear,
his greatness weighed, his will is not his own,
for he himself is subject to his birth.

KATE

Did you say something?

MICHAEL

It's a mystery to me.

BLACKOUT

END OF ACT I Scene 1

S<small>TEPHEN</small> E<small>VANS</small>

ACT I SCENE 2

Setting: The Theater

Time: A few hours later.

At Rise: Michael is seated down stage right, laptop perched on something it shouldn't be, a printer not far away.

Michael leans back in his chair, and shoots wads of paper at a hoop above a shredder. Each time he makes one we hear the shredder grinding away. He makes one, two, then misses. He gets up, retrieves it again, shoots again, and misses again. He picks up the can, sits down on the floor, and begins to cover himself with the paper.

Harry enters, carrying a large trash can.

HARRY
I met a man from the Sanitation department downstairs. If I empty this one more time, I have to join the Union.

MICHAEL

Better trash in the can than on the stage. Think
of it as a humanitarian service. You're saving
the world from this.

He uncrumples a page and reads

MICHAEL

Yesterdays, yesterdays, yesterdays

Flee in frantic folly from fickle fears

to the last earful of contorted rhyme.

HARRY

Just think: a tree died for that.

MICHAEL

I'm getting threatening phone calls from
Smokey the Bear.

HARRY

By the way, I found some books for you.
Consider it research.
Taking the paper
What does this mean?

MICHAEL

I have to write it. Do I have to know what it
means?

HARRY

I was just wondering. I think writing is
interesting.

MICHAEL

So do I. I wish I knew how it was done. I'm not
a writer, I'm a lumberjack.

HARRY

It's a little early for your 3 AM depression.

MICHAEL

Can't I go home?

HARRY

This is a theater. You are home. Besides, what
could possibly be more inspiring?

MICHAEL

A bed.

HARRY

There's one in the dressing room backstage.
You can sleep for an hour.

MICHAEL

Really?

HARRY

After you finish the first act.

MICHAEL

You're one of the good guys, Harry.

HARRY

That's what I keep telling everyone. You know
I don't like to waste time, kid. Can you at least
tell me the story?

                    MICHAEL
It's an old English legend, the story of the
Unicorn.

                    HARRY
Unicorn?

                    MICHAEL
So the story is, a young boy in the forest thinks
he sees a unicorn.

                    HARRY
Isn't that an animal?

                    MICHAEL
The kid tells his parents, who punish him for
lying.

                    HARRY
Does it have to be an animal show?

                    MICHAEL
But the kid cries and cries that he's telling the
truth.

                    HARRY
I hate animal shows.
                    MICHAEL
So, to calm him down, his parents go to see. At
first, they can't see anything.

                    HARRY
You always have to watch where you're
walking backstage.

MICHAEL

But the kid believes so strongly that soon the
parents begin to see as well.

HARRY

Besides.

MICHAEL

And when all three of them believe, the
unicorn is born into the world. Great story,
huh?

HARRY

Unicorns are expensive.

MICHAEL

Harry, the unicorn is a mythical beast.

HARRY

Great, it'll be twice as expensive. Think of
something else.

MICHAEL

There is nothing else. This is it. I'm desperate.
In all of this paper, there is not one line that is
worthy of comparison to Shakespeare. Not
one. I think we're wasting our time.

HARRY

The problem is that you are trying to write like
Shakespeare, and you can't. Shakespeare never
wrote "Shakespeare", he wrote plays. Plays
about people. You remember people.

MICHAEL

Vaguely. I'm a playwright remember. We're
not allowed out in public.

HARRY

Don't worry so much.

MICHAEL

Every time I listen to you, I end up losing
something. What am I going to lose this time?

HARRY

I don't know. What've you got left? Stop
worrying! Just do it. You been on my back for
ten years to let you write something artistic.
So now's the time.

MICHAEL

It's not that easy.

HARRY

You know why it's not easy? Because it's
impossible. You're sitting here thinking "Wow,
I've got to come with some real art." Can't be
done. You think Shakespeare did that? No
way. First, he comes up with a story. Maybe he
makes it up, maybe he steals it. Usually, he
steals it, but from somebody dead, so he's got
no problems. Then, he finds some people. He
puts the people into the story. If it's a sad
story, he finds sad people. If it's a funny story,
he finds funny people. Then, he makes sure
someone falls in love, and somebody dies,
usually from falling in love. He throws in a

witch, or maybe a fairy, then at the end he chops off someone's head. Bingo- he's got a hit. The whole process takes maybe a week. You think he labored over every line? No way. The man had deadlines.

MICHAEL
So what are you saying?

HARRY
What am I saying? I'm saying stop trying to please some dead guy. Just please yourself. I know you. I've been beating these artistic notions out of you for a long time now. As soon as I leave the room they come back, that's time-tested. Trust me. You already know what you want to be when you grow up. So be it.

MICHAEL
Okay. You know you should have been a preacher.

HARRY
I think I am. You should have been a writer.

MICHAEL
I think I am. I must have forgotten.

HARRY
So write. Stop wasting my time with questions.

Kate enters with bags of Chinese food.

                    KATE
Hi. What's going on?

                    MICHAEL
Sermon number 37.

                    KATE
I'm sorry I missed it. What was it about?

                    MICHAEL
Amnesia.

                    KATE
What?

                    HARRY
Loss. Of memory.

                    MICHAEL
Was that it?

                    HARRY
I forget.

                    KATE
Why don't you forget about that for a while
and help me with the food.

                    MICHAEL
With pleasure.

> *Kate and Michael exit. Harry walks over
> to the desk, picks up a copy of King Lear,
> and begins to read.*

HARRY

This is the excellent foppery of the world, that,

He stops reading.

when we are sick in fortune,- often the
surfeit of our own behavior- we make guilty
of our disasters the sun, the moon, and the
stars; as if we were villains by necessity,
fools by heavenly compulsion, knaves,
thieves and treachers by spherical
predominance, drunkards, liars, and
adulterers by an enforced obedience of
planetary influence; and all that we are evil
in, by a divine thrusting on.

Boy, he really hits you over the head with it,
doesn't he?

He looks offstage

Need any help? I didn't think so. That's okay.
I'm not hurt.

I'm starting to care about things. That's not
normal.

But don't give it a second thought. Don't let
the fact that I'm depressed and all alone
influence you. I don't even want you back.

Kate enters.

KATE

I'm back.

> HARRY

What?

> KATE

I'm back. I went out. And now I'm back.

> HARRY

Oh.

He laughs.

> KATE

What's so funny?

> HARRY

Wishful thinking. There's a little of that in the best of us.

> KATE

You are made of nothing else.

> HARRY

**True, I talk of dreams,
which are the children of an idle brain,
begot of nothing but vain fantasy;
which is as thin of substance as the air.**

> KATE

We've all got Shakespeare on the brain lately.

> HARRY

I must be memorizing this stuff self-consciously as I read.

> KATE

Harry, are you all right? You seem almost...human.

HARRY

It's the aging process, I guess. I feel like a fine wine in a leaky barrel.

KATE

She sits

Well, don't drip on me, please.

HARRY

There is one consolation that comes with age. You learn to see through your own illusions.

KATE

And stop trying to play on my sympathy. It's all played out.

HARRY

Wouldn't put it past me. But I know better. You need him. He needs you. And neither one of you has much use for me.

He sits next to her.

KATE

Wrong again, as usual. I need someone. He needs something. And we both happen to be standing in for the other. The past is repeating itself. It's like watching home movies, all blurry and too fast and too familiar.

HARRY

What's wrong?

KATE

I can't tell you.

HARRY

You can tell me anything. You know I never listen.

KATE

Well, in that case. When Michael and I are alone together, he looks at me as if I'm a ghost. You know, something from his past that didn't know when to leave. I want to do what's best for him. But I'm afraid that once I do, he'll be gone.

HARRY

I think we've found something in common.

KATE

It must be the end of the world.

HARRY

It's possible. Kate?

KATE

Don't say my name.

HARRY

Why not?

KATE

Because I really want someone to hold me now and I couldn't stand it if it was you.

There is a pause, in which they both stay still. Slowly, almost unconsciously, she leans her head on his shoulder. There is another pause.

KATE

I hate myself for this.

HARRY

Hate me instead. You have more practice at it.

KATE

That's the truth.

*Michael enters. They don't notice. He
stands and listens, smiling*

KATE

Harry, is he going to leave us?

HARRY

Everyone leaves everyone eventually.

KATE

Do they?

HARRY

I hope not.

KATE

You know, when you're feeling old like this, it
makes me feel young. I'm beginning to
remember things myself.

HARRY

What kind of things?

KATE

Childish things.

HARRY

Those are good things to remember. I
remember the first time I saw you. I remember
the first time I kissed you. I remember the first
time we-

KATE

Stop remembering!

HARRY

Sorry.

KATE

I suppose I should go back out and help with
the food.

Michael exits.

HARRY

I suppose you should.

A pause. No one moves.

KATE

Have I left yet?

HARRY

Afraid not.

KATE

I didn't think so. Start remembering again.
What happened to us?

HARRY

We loved not wisely but too well.

KATE

That tells me a lot.

HARRY

Actually, you never really loved me. You were just infatuated with my glamour, wealth, and good looks.

KATE

That's true.

HARRY

It is?

KATE

I don't know. It sounds familiar.

HARRY

The sad thing is you never did love me.

KATE

I never cried over any man but you.

HARRY

That's a healthy definition of love.

KATE

How would you know? No, it wasn't that I didn't love you. But even love wasn't worth getting walked over every day. I deserved better.

HARRY

I know.

KATE

I hate that. You always stop fighting just when
I get mad enough to tell the truth.

HARRY

I always did have great timing, down to the
last exquisite slam of the taxi door. Though as I
recall, it was your hand on the door handle.

KATE

Survival seemed important.

HARRY

At my age, I knew better.

KATE

At your age, it was less likely.

HARRY

You're all heart.

KATE

I was once.

HARRY

You still are.

KATE

I still am.

She laughs a little.

HARRY

What?

KATE
Shaking her head.

I'd better help with the food.

> *Pause. This time he slides*
> *unconsciously toward Kate,*
> *and they kiss.*

Have I left yet?

HARRY

No question about it. We both have. Left our
senses.

> *Getting up, breaking the*
> *mood.*

How did you do today?

KATE

Harry, I...

HARRY

From now on, you and I have one rule. We
don't hurt him.

KATE

Really?

HARRY

We're talking survival now too.

KATE

The question is whose? Damn it, I've worked
hard for this crisis. I'm entitled to it. I just
prefer to panic in private. I mean, look at me. I
have a great career, plenty of money, even
love, of a sort. Everything I'm supposed to
want. So why do I always feel so disappointed?
You want to hear paranoia? I just know that,
on my deathbed, just before I go, I'll finally

discover my reason for living. I don't think I'd mind living my life in ignorance if I thought I could die in ignorance too. But I just know that when I'm on my last legs, some joker is going to come whisper the secret of the ages in my ear. And at that moment, when it's too late, I'll know my life is a waste. That scares me more than death. But I don't know what to do about it. I'm no saint. I'm not going to spend my life in Calcutta. I think people who do are wonderful, but that's not me. And I'm no great artist. Day after day, I work with people whose talent is unimaginable to me. As human beings, you wouldn't want to meet them on the subway, but as artists, they have this gift from the universe that makes their life clear, to me at least, if not to them. But I can't run off to Tahiti to paint. I have trouble with crayons. So, what's left?

HARRY
Here's a radical thought. How about a home and a family?

KATE
Maybe that's it. Maybe it's that simple.

HARRY
From what I hear, it's not so simple.

KATE

You know what I mean. But I ask myself: is
that what they're going to whisper to me at the
end of my life? You are alive so that your
children may have life. Where is the meaning
in that? Where is the sense? Where is anything
but the mindless repetition of a biological
imperative?

HARRY

Personally, I think there's a lot to be said for
mindless repetition.

KATE

And biological imperatives, I know. But is that
why we're alive?

HARRY

Why does everyone think there has to be a
why?

KATE

We need them.

HARRY

Then make up your own.

KATE

That's something you would say. I don't mind
playing the game, I just want someone to show
me the rules.

HARRY

Don't look at me.

KATE

I can't help it. I never could. But what if. What if we're finally ready to show each other?

HARRY

You'd be wasting your time with me. Stick with him.

KATE

He doesn't want me along. And I'm not sure I want to go.

HARRY

When he says it, I'll believe it.

KATE

Will you stop being so selfless with my self? Look, maybe you owe him. But you owe me too. And some day I might collect. So just be ready. Got it?

HARRY

Yeah. I got it.

KATE

Okay, let's get down to business. Everything's set for the press conference. Have you told Michael about it yet?

HARRY

I thought I'd break it to him gradually.

KATE

How gradually?

HARRY

Now.

KATE

That's what I thought. Oh well, much ado about nothing.

HARRY

All's well that ends well.

Michael enters with food.

MICHAEL

As you like it.

HARRY

Maybe we should rehearse?

MICHAEL

I know how to eat.

KATE

He doesn't do well at press conferences.

MICHAEL

Press conferences?

HARRY

True. And this will be no ordinary press conference.

MICHAEL

We're having a press conference?

HARRY

No, we're having a press conference rehearsal.
Okay, let's set the stage. Kate, you be the
audience.

KATE

I can feel it already. A presence.

MICHAEL

I don't think I like this. I'm highly suggestible.
After I saw "Psycho", I couldn't shower alone
for weeks.

HARRY

Don't break the mood. Reach out to the other
world.

MICHAEL

Eighth avenue?

HARRY

We're having a séance. You are going to
contact the ghost of William Shakespeare.

MICHAEL

Harry, I said I'd write the play and I will. One
of these days. But I'm not going to look
ridiculous in front of a bunch of reporters. You
do it.

HARRY

It won't work that way. Kate, tell him.

KATE

It won't work that way.

HARRY

We aren't going to sell this with a lot of special effects. We'll be austere, serious, scientific. I just want you to close your eyes, sway a little bit, mumble a few unintelligible lines, then wake up and remember nothing. We just have to make them doubt their doubts a little. But it has to be you in there- calm, rational, only slightly wild about the eyes.

MICHAEL

Kate, will you explain to him that this will never work?

KATE

No.

MICHAEL

You see? What do you mean, no?

KATE

I believe it will work.

MICHAEL

You do?

HARRY

You do?

KATE

I do.

MICHAEL

Since when?

HARRY

Yes, since when?

KATE

Since a long time ago. I just forgot. Oh, I don't think anyone is really going to be fooled. But in this business, publicity is money, and this may just generate enough publicity to get it on the boards. Once that happens, who knows?

MICHAEL

You picked a fine time to figure this out.

KATE

The timing has been wrong for all three of us from the very beginning. I wanted you. Harry wanted you. I want Harry. Harry wants me. It's like daytime TV.

MICHAEL

When did all this happen?

HARRY

While you were counting the eggrolls.

MICHAEL

Well, at least it's not sudden or anything. Isn't there supposed to be a period of mourning? At least a moment of silence?

KATE

I had this thought you might be happy. For us.

MICHAEL

Someday I might be.

Dramatically.

Right now I feel like day old bread that's just been tossed in the quick sale bin of life. After all, I do love you.

KATE

How do you know?

HARRY

Yes, how <u>do</u> you know?

MICHAEL

You stay out of this. I know all about love. I've written about it dozen of times.

KATE

I'm not willing to settle for someone who's not willing to settle for me.

MICHAEL

That's not fair.

KATE

You're right. It's not fair—to me.

MICHAEL

Now let me get this straight. After spending the last ten years hating him, you spend five minutes sitting next to him and suddenly decide that it was really love after all.

HARRY

How did you know she was sitting next to me?

MICHAEL
Because. That's how things like this happen.

KATE
Michael, I love you. You know that. But I can't
help you anymore. And you can't help me.
And he needs all the help he can get.

HARRY
You're right. It is like daytime TV.

MICHAEL
So he needs you and I don't.

KATE
Right.

MICHAEL
Do you need her?

HARRY
I guess so.

MICHAEL
That's quite a declaration of love.

KATE
It's more than I ever got from you.

MICHAEL
At least you could have had the decency to run
away together. Forget that, you'd probably
want to borrow my car.

KATE
You don't have a car.

MICHAEL

That's a flimsy excuse.

KATE

We don't want to hurt you.

MICHAEL

I see no purpose in staying here any longer.

He starts to leave.

KATE

Wait.

HARRY

No. Let him go. We both know he's better off without me. This whole idea was nothing but an old man's fantasy, anyway. How important is that? Anyway, it's finished. I just wish I still had the money.

KATE

What money?

MICHAEL

Yes, what money?

HARRY

No. it's okay. I don't deserve anything from you, regardless of what happens to me.

KATE

What money?

HARRY

I'll think of a way out. That's what I'm good at.

KATE

What money?

HARRY

We had to have some front money.

MICHAEL

Harry, where did you get the money?

HARRY

Oh, hi, Mike, you still here?

MICHAEL

Yes, I'm still here. Where did you get the money?

HARRY

I—

He mumbles something.

MICHAEL

What?

HARRY

I borrowed it.

KATE

Not from?

Harry nods.

KATE

Oh Harry.

MICHAEL

When did you do this?

HARRY

You didn't really think I went to the library
did you?

KATE

This is not good.

HARRY

Things were going so well. We were finally
going to do something we could both be proud
of, something I could remember while I
rocked back and forth on the porch of my little
white house back in Kansas.

MICHAEL

Kansas? You've never been past West End
Avenue.

HARRY

Whatever. You have to look things in the eye,
no matter how devastating they may be. After
all, what's the worst that can happen?

MICHAEL

I'm afraid to think about it.

HARRY

I'll be okay. I hear Brazil is nice.

MICHAEL

Harry, pull yourself together. We'll find a way
out of this.

HARRY

We will? But how?

MICHAEL

I'll tell you how. I'm going to do this press conference, and when I'm through, they're going to believe in every ghost this side of Stephen King. So what are you waiting for? Let's get this rehearsal started.

HARRY

Okay, if you say so.

KATE

He says so.

MICHAEL

Wait a minute. First things first—I have to save the eggrolls.

Michael exits.

KATE

You are the most evil outrageous manipulative bastard I have ever met.

HARRY

My mother thanks you, my father thanks you, and I thank you.

KATE

That lie goes into your Hall of Fame.

HARRY

I'll have you know every word of that was true. Tomorrow. So you knew all along it was a lie?

KATE

Yes. And so did he.

HARRY

Really. How?

KATE

Your lips were moving. By the way, I'll lend
you the money.

HARRY

Beautiful, smart, and rich. I adore you.

*Michael enters. Harry and Kate break
quickly.*

MICHAEL

Okay, we're all set.

HARRY

Not quite.
*He unveils some fancy looking
equipment, and puts a cheap looking a
goldfish bowl on the table.*

HARRY

Now.

KATE

Impressive. What is it?

HARRY

This is highly sophisticated scientific
equipment.

                    KATE
Where'd you get it?

                    HARRY
Jake's Pawn Shop. Cost me fifty bucks.

                    KATE
What does it do?

                    HARRY
I haven't the slightest idea. But it looks
impressive.

*Harry holds up the goldfish bowl, upside
down.*

                    KATE
What is that?

                    HARRY
You can't have a séance without a crystal ball.

                    KATE
It looks like a goldfish bowl.

He holds it right-side up.

                    HARRY
This is a goldfish bowl.
        He holds it upside down.

                    HARRY
This is a crystal ball. Okay. Kate, lights.

She goes offstage. They dim.

HARRY

Remember Mike, the key is to upset their
expectations. Stay calm, cool, and scientific.
No emotion whatsoever. Got it?

MICHAEL
Mystically

I understand.

HARRY

Séance, take one. Ladies and Gentlemen of the
fourth estate, may I have your attention
please.

I come to bury Caesar, not to praise him.

KATE

Isn't that breaking the news a little soon,
Harry?

HARRY
Shaking it off

Anyway... Ladies and Gentlemen, before this
night is over, I believe you will feel like me.

KATE

Old.

HARRY

No heckling from the audience, please.

KATE

Sorry.

HARRY

Not long ago, my partner and I took refuge
from a roving band of critics who had
happened to catch our last show.

KATE

They must have been very quick. Sorry, I'm
just trying to make it realistic.

HARRY

That very night, as he hid in terror, he heard a
voice whispering to him. The voice was rich
and expressive, and spoke:

**Thus is his cheek the map of days outworn,
when beauty liv'd and died as flowers do
now,
before these bastard signs of fair were born,
and durst inhabit on a living brow,
before ... the golden tresses of the dead...**

KATE

What was that?

HARRY

I-I got carried away, I guess.

MICHAEL

This is getting spooky.

HARRY

Relax. Pay no attention to the man behind the
curtain. Where was I? Oh yeah. The voice
spoke. At first, he thought he was going crazy.

KATE

And he was right.

HARRY

But when the words started flowing from his pen...

MICHAEL

I thought I was at the keyboard.

HARRY

Who are you, Sherlock Holmes? But when the words started flowing from his *keyboard*, he knew he had been visited by none other than the ghost of William Shakespeare. And now, you are called upon to witness the revisitation of this miracle, when my associate again tries to contact the shade of the Bard of Avon.

MICHAEL

It sounds shady, all right.

HARRY

Will you get in the mood, please?

MICHAEL

Sorry. Okay.

Mystically again

I'm in the mood.

HARRY

Ladies and Gentlemen, let us put aside all doubt, all cynicism, and assist Michael as he moves into communion with the spirit world. Okay Mike, you're on. Remember, underplay.

> MICHAEL

Okay.

> *The crystal ball starts to glow.*

Hey Harry, that's pretty neat. How does it work?

> HARRY

What?

> MICHAEL

The crystal ball. How does it glow like that?

> HARRY

What are you talking about? There's no glow. I told you, that's a goldfish bowl. I borrowed it from my aunt. Poor fish died so suddenly.

> KATE

Harry, did you kill your aunt's goldfish?

> HARRY

I prefer to think of it as setting it free in the sewer.

> MICHAEL
> *Still concentrating on the
> crystal ball.*

You mean there's no glow?

> HARRY

No. You must be seeing a reflection from the lights.

> *He looks up, sees how dim the lights are,
> looks at the brightness of the bowl.*

MICHAEL
Doubtfully.
That must be it.

HARRY
Okay, start again.

MICHAEL
Right.

*At this point, smoke begins to come from
offstage.*

HARRY
What are you looking at now?

MICHAEL
The smoke.

HARRY
What smoke?

MICHAEL
Don't say what smoke! The smoke. The smoke
that is pouring out from wings. I have just one
question.

KATE
What?

MICHAEL
Do we have a fire escape?

HARRY
No, Mike, we don't want to do it this big.
Remember, underplay.

> KATE

I think he's serious.

> HARRY

He's just playing with us.

> MICHAEL

Playing. That's it. This is some method thing, isn't it? You two cooked this up so I'd know how it feels to be haunted. Well, it worked.

He leans on the equipment Harry unveiled. It flares into life, needles jumping, etc.

> MICHAEL

Harry, turn that stuff off. I don't need any more motivation.

> HARRY

I can't turn it off. It isn't on. It isn't even plugged in.

> MICHAEL

What do you mean it isn't plugged in?

He picks up the cord, stares at it.

Oh.

He starts looking around.

What the hell is going on here?

> VOICEOVER

A ghostly, booming voice

Not Hell, nor Heaven either.

MICHAEL

Oh, no.

*A wind begins to blow, and thunder
begins to sound, which only Michael
notices, naturally.*

VOICE

Michael? Michael?

MICHAEL

What? What?

HARRY

What?

MICHAEL
Shouting

What do you want?

HARRY
Shouting back

Nothing.
Pause
Why are we shouting?

VOICE

Michael?

MICHAEL

What do you want?

VOICE

You called me.

MICHAEL
Wrong number. It was a mistake. Go away.

VOICE
I am here. I have come for you.

MICHAEL
Thanks for coming. You can go now.

Michael starts looking around for the voice.

KATE
Michael, what are you doing?

MICHAEL
I'm looking for the voice. Come out. Come out, I demand to see you.

The scrim rises upstage. Smoke fills the upstage. And through the smoke, a FIGURE finally appears.

MICHAEL
Stop. I changed my mind. I don't want to see you. Go away. Be gone. Shoo.

The FIGURE steps out of the smoke. He is recognizably WillIAM SHAKESPEARE. All sound and lighting effects stop.

MICHAEL
What light through yonder window breaks?

WILL
Mortal, fear not. Your wish now grants itself.

MICHAEL
It's a dream come true.

He faints

WILL
And our little life is rounded with a sleep.

BLACKOUT

END OF ACT I

STEPHEN EVANS

ACT II SCENE 1

Setting: Same

Time: A few moments have passed.

At Rise: Harry is staring at Michael, who
                  is sitting, staring front, mouth
                  open, unable to speak. Will is at
                  this point nowhere to be seen.
                  Kate hangs up her cellphone.

KATE
Okay, it's done—no press conference.

HARRY
Good.
Pause. They watch Michael.
I think it's an improvement

KATE
You're not helping.

HARRY
He never was much of a conversationalist.

KATE
Harry!

HARRY
He could still be useful. As a coat rack, maybe,
or a hat stand.

KATE
Harry.

HARRY
Have you got a hat?

KATE
Stop it. Michael, are you okay?

MICHAEL
I...I...

HARRY
Too derivative of Beckett, I would say.

KATE
What?

MICHAEL
I...I...I...

HARRY
That's the problem with artists. So often the
symbolic becomes merely incomprehensible.

MICHAEL
I...I...I...

HARRY

Admittedly, there's a certain poetry, but what, finally, does it mean? Could you live your life on the basis of it? This reviewer doesn't think so.

MICHAEL

Will.

KATE

Will? What do you mean, Will? Will what?

MICHAEL

Yum.

HARRY

Stand back, he's going to Yum.

KATE

Harry!

MICHAEL
*As Michael re-enacts those
minutes, ad lib*

I...He...first there was...then whoosh...He...fffft...then I plllp.

HARRY

Well, I'm glad we cleared that up.

KATE

Will you be quiet? Michael, what-are-you-trying-to-tell-us?

MICHAEL

He's here.

                    KATE
He? Who? Harry? You want him to leave? I
know I want him to leave.

                    MICHAEL
No!

                    KATE
Well do you or don't you?

                    MICHAEL
No. Will.

                    HARRY
Oh no, we're back to that again.

    *Michael gathers himself, pulls them both
    close, looks around, then whispers*

                    MICHAEL
Shakespeare.

                    KATE
Yes?

                    MICHAEL
Here.

                    KATE
I give up. See what you can do.

                    HARRY
Look, you're a writer. Write it down.

    *Michael scribbles furiously and hands the
    paper to Harry.*

HARRY
Reading
The ghost of William Shakespeare was here.

He crumples the paper.

HARRY
To Kate.
Your turn again.

KATE
You're trying to tell us that you saw the ghost of William Shakespeare?
Michael nods his head.
In this room?
Michael again nods his head.
Just now?

MICHAEL
Finally breaking through
It's true.

KATE
Shakespeare.

MICHAEL
Yes. Shakespeare.
to Harry
Just like you've--
turning to Kate
Just like you've always seen him.

HARRY
We're not the ones seeing things.

KATE

Leave him alone.

HARRY

Come on. You don't mean you believe this act?
Mike, I know we should have told you about
the press conference sooner, but we just
finished making the arrangements. Honest.

MICHAEL

Harry?

HARRY

Yeah?

MICHAEL

I saw him.

HARRY

No.

MICHAEL

Yes. We've witnessed a miracle. It was
Shakespeare.

KATE

I don't think we should discuss it anymore
tonight.

HARRY

Okay, you've had a busy night. You should get
some sleep.

MICHAEL
Standing

I don't think I could sleep now. I have to
prepare my announcement to the world.

HARRY

That's okay. Kate and I will take care of it. You
lie down and be spiritual for a while. Kate,
why don't you help him lie down and I'll call
the d-o-c-t-o-r.

MICHAEL
Scornfully

Do you think Shakespeare would appear to
someone who couldn't spell?

HARRY

Sorry, I lost my head.

KATE

Harry's right. You've been under a lot of
stress, and you need some rest.

Michael lies down on something funny.
Kate covers him with something funnier.

MICHAEL

As long as you believe me.

KATE

I believe you saw something. We'll talk about
it tomorrow.

HARRY
Harry stands to the side,
watching

There is a tide in the affairs of men,
Which, taken at the flood, leads on to
fortune;
Omitted, all the voyage of their life
is bound in shallows, and in miseries.

KATE
He should sleep till morning.

HARRY
He should sleep till morning.

> *They exit. Michael gets up, pours a drink,*
> *sits at his makeshift desk. Then he sees a*
> *book.*

MICHAEL
The Legend of Sleepy Hollow.
> *He tosses it behind him and*
> *picks up the next one.*

A Christmas Carol.
> *He tosses it.*

Hamlet.
> *He tosses it, then thinks*
> *better of it. Looking toward*
> *heaven*

Sorry!
> *He picks it up. To the book.*

You met a ghost and look what happened to
you.

He looks up.

Are you or aren't you, that is the question. Am I better off insane in a simple world where everything unnatural is traced to chemical infraction? Or sane, and sane alone, in a mindless place where every rule of logic has vanished in a rush of photons on an autumn night. Tough choice. If I choose to whimper quietly in my closet for a year, tended to salvation by my friends, then I will. And everything I've seen tonight dissolves into memory. Or, if I choose, then you are real, and the life that I have known is at an end. So. Let it end.

Will appears, playing Hamlet, Sr. In a booming, ghostly voice

WILL

My hour is almost come, when I to sulphurous and tormenting flames must render up myself. I am thy father's spirit, doomed for a certain term to walk the night and for the day confined to fast in fires, till the foul crimes done in my days of nature are burnt and purged away. But that I am forbid to tell the secrets of my prison house, I could a tale unfold whose lightest word would harrow up thy soul, freeze thy young blood, make thy two eyes, like stars, start from their spheres-

MICHAEL

I believe you.

WILL
A complete change of tone

You interrupted me. Never interrupt me. You have much to learn.

MICHAEL

I'm sorry. I guess I don't know how to behave with a...whatever you are.

WILL

I see.

MICHAEL

Actually, I'm really glad you're here, because there's a question I want to ask you. Are you really here?

WILL
Booming again

You doubt me still?

MICHAEL

Not that I want you to take it personally. I just thought that as long as you are going to keep popping up, so to speak, we might as well get the social introductions out of the way. So, <u>what</u> are you?

WILL

I am as you believe.

MICHAEL

Are you a dream?

WILL
We are such stuff as dreams are made on.

MICHAEL
Clever. Did you make that up?

WILL
That is the question.

MICHAEL
Quick. You're very quick.

WILL
In truth, I am not.

MICHAEL
I see.
Pause
So. Where do we stand?

WILL
My question exactly.

MICHAEL
You mean you don't know?

WILL
Nothing is clear. I am, or was, Will
Shakespeare, born Year of Our Lord 15 and 64,
son of John Shakespeare and Mary Arden, late
of the King's Men in London.

MICHAEL
Not of an age, but for all time.

WILL
What was that?

MICHAEL

I'm sorry. I was quoting a contemporary of yours, Ben Johnson.

WILL

Beastly man. Never liked him.

MICHAEL

He must have liked you. He wrote the dedication to the first collected version of your plays.

WILL

He did what? That scoundrel had the impudence to write his name on the same page as mine? I'll...

He stops, stunned

How do you know this?

MICHAEL

I know many things about you. You were born and died on the same day, April 23. At age 18, you were married to Anne Hathaway. And in your will, you bequeathed her your second best bed. I always wondered what you meant by that.

WILL

Ah. That was a good bed. Springy, even after all those years in London. Wait. What witchcraft is this? How is it that you know these things?

MICHAEL
Not witchcraft at all. I've studied your life
since I was a child. You're taught in every
school.

WILL
Taught? You mean, remembered?

MICHAEL
You're an artistic saint, considered the greatest
playwright of all time. And, you've been a
personal hero of mine for years.

WILL
Remembered. I am remembered. How many
years?

MICHAEL
It's the year of your lord 2020.

WILL
Two score decades.
Hardly daring to ask
What of my work? Has anything been saved?

MICHAEL
Nearly all of it, I guess. 37 plays, 154 sonnets,
some longer poems.

WILL
37 plays. Did I write 37 plays?

MICHAEL
Some say yes, some no. There are 37
attributed to you.

WILL

37. They are still performed at times?

MICHAEL

More often than any other playwright, except possibly Neil Simon.

WILL

And they are well received? The public mind may now be too refined. Lust and violence may no longer interest them.

MICHAEL

They're still fairly popular.

WILL

The actors, are they well trained? They must be well trained. And the stage-it must be large, but not too large. And the entre-acts. Do they still have bear-baiting? Nothing like a good bear-baiting to keep the audience's interest up.

MICHAEL

I should have tried it with my last show.

WILL

I am remembered. Remarkable.

MICHAEL

Why remarkable? Surely you knew that your work would be preserved.

WILL

I knew it not, not cared. As a living man, I was a desperate soul, and my twisted characters mirrored my own despair. Meaning in life I

sought, and finding none, became the voice of
darkness. That's why I preferred comedy.

MICHAEL
Really? It's your tragedies that are most
famous now.

WILL
Well. They paid the bills.

MICHAEL
I have to ask. Which was your favorite play?

WILL
The best is no doubt is A Midsummer Night's
Dream.

MICHAEL
That's my favorite!

WILL
My favorite is probably As You Like It. And
anything with Falstaff.

He begins to reminisce.

WILL
Ah Rosalind. She was real, though I never met
her in life. I wrote my sonnets for her as well.
In her youth she dressed as a man. As she grew
older, she grew darker. But still.

MICHAEL
Why have you come back? Why are you here?

WILL

To work. Here can I pour my anguished heart, and so eviscerate a while the dark. For if life was a shadow, death is darker still. I could not work. I could not create. My work was all I had on earth. No longer could I be without.

MICHAEL

You couldn't work?

WILL

Only God creates from nothing, boy. In heaven, there's naught but cold unyielding glory. A darker beauty calls to me. Less lofty, mayhap, but more human. Death. Life. Love. Laughter-there is none in heaven. No laughter. No hope-for hope requires change. Nothing a man can know as beautiful. Heaven is for angels, boy, and saints, and I am neither. So was I sent back. So am I here, returned for one night unto this sphere to find perhaps a trace of hope in beauty, laughter, love in life, enough to last eternity.

MICHAEL

You speak just as I imagine.

WILL

Indeed, exactly as you imagine. The words are from your mind. All that you see and hear of me is framed by your thoughts, so that you may believe and understand. To speak. To pronounce once more this glorious language is

a joy I thought forever lost. Even this
barbarous version stolen from your mind.

MICHAEL

One night?

WILL

One.

MICHAEL

Why me? What made you choose me?

WILL

I did not choose you, though perhaps you were
chosen. This I know: I can appear only to
another poet, another artist. Perhaps your
spirit was kindred to my own.

MICHAEL

**Oh, how I faint when I of you do write,
Knowing a better spirit doth use your name,
And in the praise thereof spends all his
might,
To make me tongue-tied, speaking of your
fame!**

WILL

Sorry.

MICHAEL

What? Wait a minute. Did you do that?

WILL

Yes. My presence draws from weaker minds
the words that I have written.

MICHAEL

That's why we were going around quoting
Shakespeare, I mean, quoting you,
unexpectedly?

WILL
Excitedly

But come, at last, to work. We must be done
by morning. For by the light of day, I shall be
but a whisper of your dream. Write as I
instruct.

MICHAEL

I can't.

WILL

Centuries have I waited for this—you can't?

MICHAEL

No.

WILL
Puzzled

You can't?

MICHAEL

No.

WILL
Upset

You can't?

MICHAEL

No.

WILL

Angry

You can't?

MICHAEL

No.

WILL

Furious

You can't?

MICHAEL

No.

WILL

Calm

I see.

Exploding

Why can't you?

MICHAEL

I can't tell you.

Same pattern again.

WILL

You can't tell me?

MICHAEL

No.

WILL

You can't tell me?

MICHAEL

No.

WILL
You can't tell me?

MICHAEL
No.

WILL
You can't tell me?

MICHAEL
No.

WILL
You can't tell me?

MICHAEL
No.

WILL
I see.
Pause
Why can't you tell me?

MICHAEL
I don't know.

WILL
Starting again
You don't know?

MICHAEL
Please don't start that again.

WILL
What madness is this? This is your dream.

MICHAEL
I know. I'm sorry.

WILL

The miracle shall be lost, and I condemned to
silence everlasting.

MICHAEL

I'm sorry. I'd really like to help you. But I just
can't.

WILL

We are so alike, my young friend. In every
face, we see the hidden thoughts. In every
smile, fear. In every curse, desire. Nothing
human hides from us, but us. I know your fear.
It is the true haunting of your life.

MICHAEL

You know, my Dad called me 'Shakespeare'.
He didn't know. I was the first kid in my class
to need glasses, and the first on
antidepressants. Anyway, by the time I got to
college, even you would have had a hard time
living up to my expectations. I had no chance
at all. I'd written a play. The school agreed to
produce it during a festival featuring new
works. If it wasn't special enough, then that
would be it.

WILL

Quietus with a bare bodkin.

MICHAEL

More likely a bottle of pills. And then I met
Harry. Harry was perfect for me, the perfect

excuse never to face myself. You know,
everyone thinks that he used me.
              Michael laughs
Not true. I used him, and Kate, and anyone
else I had to. All that mattered was keeping the
illusion that someone else was to blame for
what I never did—for what I was afraid I
couldn't do. The funny thing is, on the night
when that illusion goes berserk, on the night
when the real God of the Theater comes to
sweep me off to Broadway paradise, on this
night, I can finally grow up and face the truth.
I'm not you. I can't ever be you. Or probably
anything close. And I'm through trying. I don't
want those comparisons anymore. I want to be
free. Free to be content with myself. Finally.

                    WILL
And what if I told you...

                    MICHAEL
Don't. Please.

                    WILL
Then I won't.

                    MICHAEL
              Pause
Tell me what?

WILL

Do you think I haven't felt the fear you feel? I
have. I feel it even now. You cannot learn how
not to fail. The body fails. So does the mind.
But you can learn to value your success.

MICHAEL

What do you mean?

WILL

I have learned something of eternity. Nothing
lasts forever in itself. But what you create, also
creates. And this does last, untraceable as the
elements after death. So what you create
continues to reverberate through life and time,
from mind to mind, forever. In truth, what
else am I?

MICHAEL

I wish I could believe you.

WILL

Believe this. An artist does one simple thing—
he arcs the void, as I have reached to you. If
you do this, no matter in how brief or small a
way, then you have achieved all a human can.
And this is within the grasp of everyone. Your
own creation is your own reward.

MICHAEL

I'm not sure how I'll feel in the morning. But
now—let's work.

                    WILL
Lay on, Macduff.

       Michael looks at Will
       expectantly.

Et cetera.

  BLACKOUT

  END OF ACT II Scene 1

ACT II SCENE 2

Setting: The theater.

Time: Morning.

At Rise: Will gazes longingly at the
champagne bottle. He sighs.

WILL

The intensity of sense is what I miss. A good-
sherris sack hath a two-fold operation in it. It
ascends me into the brain; dries me there all
the foolish and dull and crudy vapours which
environ it; makes it apprehensive, quick,
forgetive, full of nimble fiery and delectable
shapes; which, delivered over to the voice, the
tongue, which is the birth, becomes excellent
wit. The second property of your excellent
sherris is, the warming of the blood...

He looks offstage

WILL

If I had a thousand sons, the first human
principle I would teach should be, to forswear
thin potations and to addict themselves to
sack.

*Kate enters. Will's attention immediately
turns to her.*

WILL
Age cannot whither her, nor custom stale her
infinite variety;

*Harry enters, stumbling in, disheveled
and unready for the morning.*

WILL
Other women cloy the appetites they feed, but
she makes hungry where most she satisfies

*Kate and Harry look at each other. It is
apparent that their relationship has
taken another step. They pause and look
at each other.*

HARRY
Good morning.

KATE
Good morning.

HARRY
Sleep well?

KATE
Yes. You?

HARRY
Better than I have in about 15 years. Is he up?

KATE

Apparently not. I thought I heard him, though.
I wonder how he's doing?

HARRY

Probably better than we are. At least he had a
good night's sleep.

KATE

I'm worried about him.

HARRY

That's silly. Last night he was having a little
fun with us. We'll all laugh about it this
morning over breakfast.

KATE

I hope so.

Michael enters, eyes glazed.

MICHAEL
To Harry

Good morning.
To Kate

Good morning.
To Will

Good morning.
To all

You want coffee? I made coffee. You need
coffee? I need coffee. I'll get coffee.

Michael exits.

KATE

He said good morning three times. He said it
to you. He said it to me. Then he said it again.

HARRY

Double vision.

KATE

Then he'd have said it four times.

HARRY

One and a half vision.

KATE

Is that like having half a brain?

HARRY

He was sleepy. It was a mistake.

KATE

I guess.

*Michael enters, bringing four cups. He
gives one to Harry, one to Kate, one to
Will.*

WILL
Refusing
It's a bit too late for me.

MICHAEL

You mean too early.

WILL

No, too late. By about four centuries.

MICHAEL

Ah, right.

KATE

What?

MICHAEL

What? Did you say something?

KATE

I said what.

MICHAEL

What? What?

KATE

What?

HARRY

This is beginning to sound like Morse code.
Did you say something?

MICHAEL

I said what.

HARRY

That's what I want to know. What did you say?

MICHAEL

What.

KATE

Yes, what?

WILL

What, what!

MICHAEL
What? Wait. Whoa.

HARRY
What?

KATE
Wait.

WILL
Well!

MICHAEL
Will!

KATE
Who?

MICHAEL
What? Oh, I'm sorry. Kate, Harry, Will. Will, Kate, Harry.

HARRY
Will we what?

MICHAEL
No. Will.

KATE
Wait. Why-are you drinking two cups of coffee?

MICHAEL
Because it's too late.

KATE
For what?

MICHAEL

For coffee.

Pause

That doesn't make any sense, does it?

They stare at him

I'm going to the dressing room to get cleaned up. We'll discuss this later. Oh.

Michael picks up a sheaf of papers and hands it to Harry

MICHAEL

This is for you. I'll be right back.

KATE

That is a seriously disturbed person. He's definitely not the same person he was yesterday.

HARRY

Who is?

KATE

Harry, what if it happened because of us?

HARRY

Us?

KATE

Yes, us. It's been known to happen. I read about it in the New York Post. What if he just couldn't handle it and went over the edge?

WILL

It's possible.

KATE

Maybe he really was in love with me after all.
And the way he sees it, we betrayed him. It
could make anyone crazy.

WILL

Ah, the plot.

KATE

Think! How would he react?

WILL

He'd cut off their heads.

KATE

He wouldn't get violent.

WILL

Too bad.

KATE

That's not his style. No. He'd dive into the
nearest fantasy.

WILL

Fantasy. I like that.

KATE

One that you and I neatly provided.

WILL

We'll need some witches.

KATE

One that would solve all the problems we
caused.

WILL

And maybe a few fairies.

KATE

Shakespeare would appear and be his personal
savior, to save him from himself, and us.

WILL

That works for me.

KATE

Harry, that's what happened. I'm sure of it.
And we're responsible. So it's up to us to do
something about it.

HARRY

Like what?

KATE

It's going to mean a sacrifice.

WILL

Human?

KATE

First, we'll have to explain to him that there's
nothing between us.

HARRY

There isn't? I could have sworn there was.

KATE

There is. But that's something he can never
know.

HARRY

Lying. I can handle that.

KATE

Second, we can't talk about this play, or
writing, or Shakespeare. Not for a very long
time.

HARRY

What about my idea?

KATE

Harry, do you really think it would have
worked?

HARRY

I suppose not. How could he write a play that
sounded like Shakespeare?

WILL

There are more things in heaven and earth,
Harry, than are dreamt of in your philosophy.

HARRY

Yeah, I guess it's for the best.

*Harry looks at the manuscript and reads,
gradually getting more and more excited.*

KATE

It will be difficult for both of us. But we have
to be strong, for his sake. We'll have to go for
long walks in the park with him, maybe move
to the country. You don't think they'll have to
hospitalize him, do you? I couldn't stand to see
that. But you know what the hardest part will
be? Not letting him see anything between us.

HARRY
looking at the manuscript

I don't believe it.

KATE

It's true. No looking deep into my eyes. No
brushing my cheek with your fingers, or
smoothing my hair, or running your hand...

HARRY

This is it!

Harry runs to Kate and kisses her wildly.

KATE

No, Harry, we can't. We have to be strong.
He kisses her again.
No, strong, we can't. We have to be Harry.

*He drops her suddenly, looking amazed
at the manuscript.*

HARRY

He did it. He really did it.

KATE

Harry, I cannot deal with two crazy people at
once.

HARRY

I always knew he could do it. I never doubted
him for a minute. Don't you understand? The
play. He wrote it in one night. But that's not
the amazing thing. The amazing thing is, it's
brilliant.

WILL

Naturally. Or perhaps, supernaturally.

HARRY

I could almost believe Shakespeare came back from the dead to write it.

WILL

There are more things in heaven and earth... wait, I already said that.

KATE

Let me see it.

HARRY

And he did it in one night. I always knew he was a genius. You know what? We're going to be rich. As in having lots and lots of money. Rich!

WILL

Rich!

KATE

No, we're not.

HARRY

We're not?

WILL

We're not?

KATE

No.

HARRY

Why not?

WILL

Yes, why not?

KATE

What are you thinking of?

HARRY

I'm thinking of getting rich. What are you
thinking of?

KATE

We have a man in there whose mental welfare
is hanging by a thread. This play proves how
disturbed he is.

WILL

I beg your pardon.

KATE

Even if it was good, and I don't see how it
could be if he wrote it in one night, we can't
ever let him see it or hear about it again.

*Harry looks at her. Then at the
manuscript. Then back at her.*

HARRY

But...

KATE

Don't you see? It could be the final shock that
does him in, and we may never reach him
again.

*Harry looks at her. Then at the
manuscript. Then back at her.*

                        HARRY
But...

    She takes the manuscript.

                        KATE
Harry, we have to get rid of it. Pretend it never
existed.

    He takes it back.

                        HARRY
Now you're the one who is acting crazy. We're
talking about a million dollars here. Maybe ten
million dollars.

                        WILL
How much is that in shillings?

                        KATE
You know, every time I start to feel some hope
for you, we always get back to money. Isn't his
health and sanity worth more than a few
dollars?

                        HARRY
It isn't the money. Okay, partly it's the money.
But don't you see? It's the idea. It could work.
Do you know how seldom that happens
nowadays? I can't throw that away.

KATE

You have two choices, Harry. You can walk
out the door with that manuscript and never
come back. Or you can shred it and stay here
with me. What's it going to be?

*Pause. Will, shocked by the whole turn of
events, looks on with horror. Harry looks
at Kate, then at the play. He walks
quickly to the front door.*

KATE

Harry!

HARRY

Just kidding. Never thought I'd turn out to be
such a sap.

*Harry moves toward the
shredder*

Do I hafta?

KATE

You hafta.

He starts to move again. Kate stops him

KATE

Harry. Thanks.

HARRY

For you.

*Harry reluctantly drops the manuscript
in the shredder. Will lets out a   ·
bloodcurdling scream. Michael run in.*

MICHAEL
What the hell is going on here?

WILL
Horror beyond belief.

KATE
Nothing. What do you mean?

MICHAEL
I heard...

KATE
I told you, nothing. You should get some sleep.

MICHAEL
It's morning.

KATE
Oh. Right. Good morning.

MICHAEL
Sleep well?

Harry   Kate
Yes. No.   No. Yes.

MICHAEL
I see.

He turns to Will
I can't get a straight Answer out of them. How
about you?

WILL
The last hundred years were a little restless.

MICHAEL
That's not what I mean.

KATE

Michael, don't.

MICHAEL

Quiet, please. I'm trying to have a
conversation.

KATE

Michael, please don't do this to yourself. We
aren't worth it.

MICHAEL

I'll get back to that later.

KATE

Michael, there's no one there.

HARRY

Where is there?

MICHAEL
He points to Will

There. And I'm beginning to wish it were true.
This is going to be a problem. Wait. I can
prove to you that he's real.

*Michael looks for the
manuscript.*

Where'd it go?

WILL
Still in disbelief

They beheaded it.

Michael lets out a scream.

That's what I said.

MICHAEL
You didn't?

WILL
Yes, I did. It sounded just like yours.

HARRY
On a whole different track
No, we didn't. How did you know?

MICHAEL
How could you do it?

KATE
Kicking Harry
How could we do what?

MICHAEL
How could you do... what you did?

KATE
We thought it was the best thing for you.

HARRY
We did?

MICHAEL
Oh. You did. Both of you. Together. My two
best friends. And you did it behind my back.

HARRY
Well, we weren't going to do it in front of you.

KATE
Harry, shut up. It was an accident.

HARRY
It was?

MICHAEL
How could it be an accident?

KATE
To Harry
I don't think you should say anymore.

MICHAEL
Just tell me it isn't true.

HARRY
I can't. I have to be honest.

KATE
Since when?

HARRY
Kate and I slept together last night.

MICHAEL
I knew that.

HARRY
I know it's a shock.

KATE
You knew that?

HARRY
I told you he knew. How'd you know?

MICHAEL
I don't care about that. I'm talking about
something serious.

KATE
And my sleeping with Harry isn't? You are
crazy.

MICHAEL

Look, whatever you two did last night is okay
with me. I'm all for it. I was just pretending to
be upset because I didn't want you to think I
didn't care.

KATE

What?

MICHAEL

I mean I thought we needed to have a serious
discussion about the future of our relationship.

KATE

I'll tell you what your future is...

Harry holds her back

MICHAEL

Stop trying to change the subject. I want to
know why you beheaded, I mean shredded,
my manuscript.

HARRY

How did you know we shredded it? We never
said that.

MICHAEL

I have friends in high places.

HARRY

It's getting weird again.

MICHAEL

I want to know why you shredded my play. It
was the answer to everything. For all of us.

KATE

All four of us?

MICHAEL

As a matter of fact, yes.

KATE

Michael, sit down here. You're right. We have to talk.

Michael sits next to her.

I know that what has happened, what we've done, has hurt you.

*Michael starts to say
something.*

Please don't deny it.

He tries again.

Please. Let me finish. I know that we've hurt you. And I know that hurt has caused you to seek refuge in this fantasy. I'm not going to argue with you. I just want you to know that what happened between Harry and me last night is over, and it will never happen again. From now on, I'm going to dedicate my life to making you well.

We did shred your play, I admit it. And I know it was a terrible thing to do. But we had no choice. As long as it was around, you'd never let go of your fantasy world. You'll write other plays, better ones, once you come back to the real world. I know you can't do it all at once. But someday, you will. And I'll be with you.

                    HARRY
And I won't.

                    MICHAEL
What?

                    HARRY
I've hurt you enough, kid. I've taken
everything you had to give, until all that's left
is a deluded husk of a man.

                    MICHAEL
Who are you calling a husk?

                    HARRY
I've taken the wheat and thrown the chaff
away into the gutter and watched it wash
down the wrong side of the street, mixing with
the dirt and the grime and the refuse until it
becomes a filthy worthless inhuman...

                    MICHAEL
I get the picture.

                    HARRY
Sorry. Anyway, I'm leaving. You'll both be
better off without me around to screw things
up.

                    MICHAEL
Time out here. This isn't what I planned. Just
let me think for a minute.

    He moves away.

WILL

Plot problems? I hate those.

MICHAEL

I don't get it. This could have been the greatest
night of my life. I had everything I ever
wanted. I met William Shakespeare. I wrote
the play of my dreams. I was inches away from
fame, fortune, American Express commercials.

MICHAEL

And now everything has fallen apart. Kate is
leaving Harry for me. Harry is leaving, period.
And the play is gone. My finest work is now
ticker tape. My life is over.

WILL

Dramatic, but unconvincing.

MICHAEL

What do you mean?

WILL

I know that you have a copy of the play on
your clever device. Why pretend otherwise? I
wrote this scene, remember? Henry IV, Part 2.
Prince Hal rids himself of the loyal Falstaff,
leaves the friends who supported him in his
youth, ascends to the crown and lives
gloriously ever after as King Henry V. Falstaff
of course dies of loneliness and cruelty, but
such is the price of kingship.

MICHAEL
That can't be me.

WILL
Fate has taken reign and delivered your
desires.

MICHAEL
I wouldn't do that.

WILL
Make not the mistakes I made!

MICHAEL
Would I? I mean, without them, it means
nothing. I need them. I need them both. I can't
believe I'm saying this. Great. Thank you for
pointing out how much I need them just when
I'm about to lose them both. Harry's still going
to leave. Kate still thinks I'm crazy. And she'll
go on burning every copy of the play I can put
together, until she's convinced otherwise.

WILL
That is a problem.

MICHAEL
There's only one solution. They have to
believe in you.

WILL
It seems the only answer.

MICHAEL
Great.

WILL

Unfortunately it's impossible.

MICHAEL

It can't be impossible. It happened to me.
There must be some way for them to see you,
too.

WILL

You and I are artists. Our spirits are in
harmony. That is why you see, and why they
cannot.

MICHAEL

I don't understand.

WILL

Your heart and mine found meaning in
creation, the life of beauty, the service of the
art. But what answer is true for every man? On
either side of death, I know of none. Each
must choose his own, or else have none. If
their choice be not the match and complement
to mine, some other spirit may answer. But I
may not.

MICHAEL

I believe you are the truth. And I believe they
need to share that truth. And I can't believe
that something so real and meaningful to me
cannot touch them as well.

*All this time, Harry and Kate have
observed this conversation, though to*

*them it appears Michael is talking to the
air. Kate breaks down, and Harry tries to
comfort her, though he is greatly pained
himself. Michael goes to Harry and Kate.*

MICHAEL
Look. Look at these two people.

KATE
Michael, don't do this.

MICHAEL
Are you saying you have nothing to give to
them? I don't believe it. These are the people
you were writing for all along. You didn't
write for the scholars who count up the
number of times you wrote the word 'moon'.
Or the actors who stammer out your speeches
or the directors who twist your plays in the
name of creativity. You wrote for people just
like them. Maybe they are ordinary. I mean,
God knows, Harry's a liar, a cheat, and a thief,
and that's just for starters.

HARRY
That's not fair. If I say I'm not a cheat, that
makes me a liar.

MICHAEL

And Kate. You have always known the truth
about us. You have dedicated your life to two
men who have dedicated their lives to hurting
you. Here we are, the saint, the clown, and the
villain, three perfect players come to life.
What would you have us do, master
playwright? I'll tell you this. If you cannot
reach their hearts, you'll have none of mine.

WILL

So you think I need motivation, do you? Some
incentive to shake four hundred years of rust?

MICHAEL

I'm sorry. I should realize I can't manipulate
you. Habit, I guess. The real truth is, I needed
you but didn't deserve you. They need you,
and do.

WILL

Vision is birth. It requires pain. Their need is
great, that is plain enough. But I see no hope.

*Will begins to walk around as if studying
them. He stops at Harry. Harry follows
Michael's eyes following Will and begins
to get nervous.*

MICHAEL

Try.

HARRY

Stop looking at what I'm not seeing.

WILL

Very well. First we must make them doubt
their doubts. We must create the question in
their minds. I believe I know a way.

MICHAEL

Go ahead.

Will gestures to Harry.

HARRY

Mike, this is ridiculous.
                    Harry turns to Kate
Will you please tell him-

**The brain of this foolish-compounded clay,
man,**
**is not able to invent anything that tends to
laughter,**
more than I invent or is invented on me:
**I am not only witty in myself, but the cause
that wit is in other men.**

KATE

How did you-
                    Will gestures to Harry.
**Pale as his shirt, his knees knocking each
other;**
and with a look so piteous in purport
as if he had been loosed out of Hell
to speak of horrors, he comes before me.

MICHAEL

Mad for thy love?

KATE
My Lord, I do not know;
But truly I do fear it.

Hypnosis. Or something, I don't know. I won't believe in ghosts.

HARRY
I will.

WILL
Yes. The potential for alignment now exists. The doubt and the desire are there. But that is not enough.

HARRY
I think I see something.

WILL
Only another creative mind can make the final link.

HARRY
I hear something too.

WILL
Only an artist's soul can apprehend my visage.

HARRY
It's him!

WILL
Silence! He interrupts more than you.

HARRY
Sorry.

Will and Michael realize that Harry can now see and hear Will.

MICHAEL
We may have to revise your theory.

WILL
It can't be. Only an artist. I'm sure.

HARRY
What's he upset about?

MICHAEL
You're not supposed to be able to see him. You're not an artist.

HARRY
Some people consider me an artist.

MICHAEL
Who?

HARRY
'Fingers' Morgan. 'Loose Lips' Louie...

MICHAEL
We're not talking about con artists.

WILL
Yes, we are.

HARRY
You know 'Loose Lips'?

WILL

There are many kinds of artists, are there not?
Some work in stone, some sound, some light.
And some there are that only work in dreams.
Often they fail, as dreams are wont to do. But
for all that, their craft is true and worthy of the
name of art. The dreamer reads the mind of
God. Here is no master of the craft. But the
dream that we now live was born in the
laughter of your heart. As your creation, we
dream, and we endure.

HARRY

I feel like I've lived my whole life in Kansas,
and I just jumped over the rainbow.

All three turn to look expectantly at Kate.

MICHAEL
To Will

You're two for two. Care to try for three?

KATE

You're both crazy and I'm leaving.

HARRY AND MICHAEL

No!

HARRY

Kate, you have to trust me on this. One last
time. All or nothing.

Kate turns away.

KATE

I don't know what to believe anymore. Maybe Shakespeare's ghost is zooming around the room at this very minute. It doesn't matter. Don't you understand? I'm a normal person. I need normal things. I don't need to write great plays or make up fancy schemes. I just need someone to love. And someone to love me. And I'm not even sure anymore that they need to be the same person. I'll take what I can get. But I can't get it here.

Will laughs.

WILL

I understand. Fear not. We shall reach her. For hers is the noblest art of all, the art that forms in flesh and shapes our souls. This also did I miss on earth. In binding flesh, we bound the universe. What we create cannot compare with this: life gets love, so love gets life. And the life that's now within grows in that love.

So long as men can breathe, or eyes can see,

So long lives this, and this gives life to thee.

Kate stays very still, as if listening. Will whispers something to her. Slowly, she turns to look at Will, and smiles.

KATE

Thank you.

HARRY

What did he say?

KATE

This were to be new made when thou art old,
And see thy blood warm when thou feel'st it
cold.

WILL

Walking to the laptop

Well put. 'Tis why I was sent back. I had to see
that I have moved beyond. 'Twas you who
knew. Some other work there is that beckons.
A different beauty calls, an eternity to create.
That is heaven.

*Will passes his hand over the
laptop*

Alas, my friends, The gloworm shows the
matins to be near, and 'gins to pale his
ineffectual fire. Adieu. Adieu. Hamlet,
remember me.

MICHAEL

It waves me still. Go on, I'll follow thee.

WILL

No! You are released to your own voice, as I
am to mine. You will know what to say.

MICHAEL

Do you hafta?

WILL

I hafta.

MICHAEL
Go on. I'll follow thee.

KATE
How can we ever thank you?

WILL
The chance of meeting you has paid all debt.

HARRY
If you're ever in the market for a producer...

WILL
Yes?

HARRY
I'll make a few calls.

Will moves to Michael.

MICHAEL
Is this the end?

WILL
In other space and time, perhaps we may yet
meet again.

*Will walks upstage. The
smoke begins to rise. He
turns.*

...Now I want Spirits to enforce, art to enchant:
And my ending is despair, Unless I be relieved
by prayer, Which pierces so that it assaults
Mercy itself and frees all faults. As you from
crimes would pardon'd be, Let your
indulgence set me free.

Will disappears.

HARRY
I've always admired a good exuent.

KATE
That's an art you'll have to forget.

MICHAEL
I'll drink to that.

They break out the champagne.

KATE
*Kate starts to drink, but
changes her mind*
No, I'd better not.
Michael runs to the laptop.
Michael, what are you doing?

MICHAEL
I have to see if it's still there.

KATE
What?

MICHAEL
The play.

HARRY
Please, please, please tell me it is.

Michael stops, puzzled.

MICHAEL
It's gone.

HARRY
Pushing lots of buttons
You must be pushing the wrong buttons.

MICHAEL
No. He said it. I am released to my own voice.

HARRY
Oh. Too bad. But never mind that. I've got an idea that's even better.

KATE
No!

HARRY
Kate, this is different. You'll love this one. It's about these two guys who try this scam about writing a play by Shakespeare...

MICHAEL
Shaking his head
It'll never work.

KATE
Sorry, you'll be much too busy...

HARRY
Why?

KATE
Taking care of our child...

HARRY
Who?

KATE
At our beach house in Malibu...

HARRY
Where?

KATE
After I take that studio job...

HARRY
What?

KATE
While you retire and write your memoirs.

HARRY
When?

KATE
Which ought to be worth a hefty advance...

HARRY
Eyes starting to glow
How?

KATE
If you have the right agent. And I'd say that
you do.

HARRY
You may have something there.

KATE
I'd say that I do.

HARRY
But how...
Pause
Aren't you going to interrupt me?

KATE

Harry, I would never interrupt you...

HARRY

But...

KATE

As long as I've finished speaking. Equal time?

HARRY

We'll negotiate.

KATE

I'll look forward to it. Now as you were
saying...

HARRY

But how...
                Cautious
about Michael?

KATE

Yes, how about it, Michael? Harry's memoirs.
Ever thought of being a ghost writer?

MICHAEL

It's what I live for.
                To the Audience
**Ours be your patience then, and yours our
parts,**
**Your gentle hands lend us, and take our
hearts.**

                He looks up
All's Well.

BLACKOUT

END OF PLAY

PLAYWRIGHT'S NOTE

The lines in **boldface** are quotations from Shakespeare. They are distinguished from other Shakespearean quotes in the play in that the characters are compelled to say them.

The lines may be accompanied by a lighting change to indicate a supernatural effect. The lines should be spoken in natural rhythms and inflections, and should blend with the character's natural speech. Only after they have said the lines should the characters realize they have uttered something strange

STEPHEN EVANS

ACKNOWLEDGEMENTS

The Ghost Writer was first produced in 1990 by the Annapolis Theater Project in Annapolis, MD. It was produced again in 1991 by the Guerilla Theater in Kansas City, Kansas, and again in 2013 by Theater 11 in Annapolis, MD.

STEPHEN EVANS

ABOUT THE PLAYWRIGHT

Stephen Evans is a playwright and the author of *A Transcendental Journey, Painting Sunsets,* and *The Island of Always.* Find him online at:

https://www.istephenevans.com/

https://www.facebook.com/iStephenEvans

https://twitter.com/iStephenEvans

STEPHEN EVANS

BOOKS BY STEPHEN EVANS

Fiction:

The Marriage of True Minds

Let Me Count the Ways

The Island of Always

Two Short Novels

Painting Sunsets

The Mind of a Writer and other Fables

Non-Fiction:

A Transcendental Journey

Funny Thing Is: A Guide to Understanding Comedy

The Laughing String: Thoughts on Writing

Layers of Light

Liebestraum

Plays:

The Ghost Writer

Spooky Action at a Distance

Tourists

Generations (with Morey Norkin and Michael Gilles)

The Visitation Quartet

As You Like It (Adaptation)

Verse:

Sonets from the Chesapeke

A Look from Winter

Limerosity

Limerositus

STEPHEN EVANS

Lightning Source UK Ltd.
Milton Keynes UK
UKHW010703101022
410232UK00004B/456